The Old Man
Who Loved to Sing

John Winch

Scholastic Inc.

New York

In a secluded valley, far from the city,
lived an old man who loved to sing.

When he wasn't singing he whistled, and when he wasn't whistling he played music on an old wind-up gramophone.

He usually did all three very, very loudly.

The old man had once lived in the city, but there came a time when he could no longer hear himself sing above the noise.

At first, the unfamiliar sounds of his music
echoing through the valley disturbed the animals.

But soon they came to love the music.

At night, when the old man fell asleep in his armchair,
the animals would gather around his campfire.

As the years passed, the old man grew forgetful,
as people sometimes do;
much to the delight of the sparrows . . .

and the possum . . .

and the wombats.

Sometimes he forgot to eat his lunch, but it never went to waste.

One day he forgot to sing. He forgot to whistle.
He even forgot to play music on the old wind-up gramophone.

The old man knew something was missing,
but he could not remember what it was.

Without the sound of the old man's music,
the valley became silent.

The kangaroos, disturbed by the silence,
began to beat their tails softly in the dust.
The sound of their drumming carried . . .

down to the creek where the frogs joined in with loud, throaty croaks.

The birds heard their call and burst into song.

Soon the valley echoed with singing.

But the loudest song of all came from . . .

the old man.

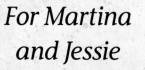

*For Martina
and Jessie*

All rights reserved. Published by Scholastic Inc., 555 Broadway, New York,
NY 10012 by arrangement with Ashton Scholastic Pty Limited.
SCHOLASTIC HARDCOVER is a registered trademark of Scholastic Inc.,
555 Broadway, New York, NY 10012.

Library of Congress Cataloging-in-Publication Data available
    Library of Congress number: 95-5307
    ISBN 0-590-22640-1

12 11 10 9 8 7 6 5 4 3 2 1   6 7 8 9/9 1 0/0

Printed in Singapore   46
First printing, April 1996

Typeset in Stone Informal
The illustrations in this book were painted in gouache and watercolor.

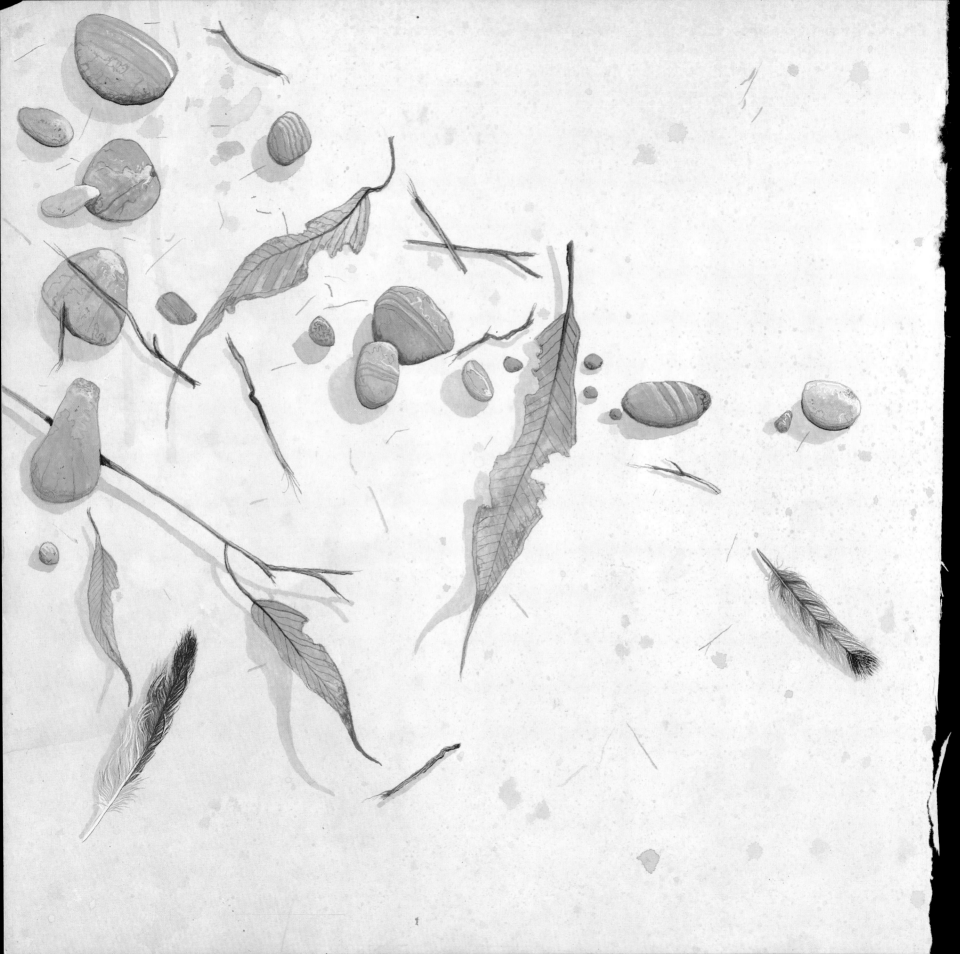